Dear
Mr President

For Emile, Oliver and Lilka, who all know
what it's like to share a room! – SS

For Willian, Nathan, Alexis and Maxime – AV

A TEMPLAR BOOK

First published in New Zealand in 2018 by Millwood Press.
This paperback edition first published in the UK in 2019 by Templar Books,
an imprint of Bonnier Books UK,
The Plaza, 535 King's Road, London, SW10 0SZ
www.templarco.co.uk
www.bonnierbooks.co.uk

Text copyright © 2018 by Sophie Siers
Illustration copyright © 2018 by Anne Villeneuve

1 3 5 7 9 10 8 6 4 2

ISBN: 978-1-78741-519-5

This book was typeset in Clue
The illustrations were created with watercolour

Printed in Latvia

Dear
Mr President

Sophie Siers
Anne Villeneuve

templar
books

Dear Mr President,

I'm writing you a letter from my bedroom on the other side of the world. Sadly, the room does not belong only to me. I have to share it with my big brother who exactly fits your description of an undesirable person.

I watched you on the TV news tonight and you said you were building a wall. It made me think that perhaps I need one too.

Yours faithfully,

Sam

Dear Mr President,

The problem is that my brother has a phone and he plays on it at night even though he isn't allowed. It keeps me awake. I suggested to Mum and Dad that they let me build a wall across the room.

They said no.

Very sincerely,

Sam

Dear Mr President,

At dinner tonight we had a discussion about the wall proposals, both yours and mine. I don't know about you, but I'm getting a lot of negative feedback.

My brother said that they're both dumb ideas.

Mum said that if you were like other men she knew you would talk about it a lot but never build it.

Dad didn't say anything.

Respectfully,

sam

Dear Mr President,

Everybody was talking about your wall at school today.
There didn't seem to be many kids who thought it was a good idea.

They obviously don't know what it's like to share a room.

Our teacher, Mr Green, has set us a project on 'Great Walls of the World'. He said that some of them didn't quite work to plan. I told him that mine definitely would!

Yours truly,

Sam

Dear Mr President,

Dad took my brother and me fishing today.
He wanted to talk about the wall.

He said we needed to talk things over and see if we
could 'negotiate' a way to make things work in our room.
I told him that actions speak louder than words.

I thought that's the sort of thing you'd say in my situation.

Best regards,

sam

Dear Mr President,

I've discovered I'm great at building walls! I've built two in the garden and one that went right across the pond that made a dam as well. I made them out of sand and stones and Dad said my best one looked like the Great Wall of China!

He told me that it was the biggest wall ever made and was built to hold back marauding invaders.

It sounds like just what I need.

Your friend,

Dear Mr President,

My brother is behaving like a marauding invader.
This morning he took my spaceship.
That means war.

I told my mum that this could have been averted
if she had let me build a wall but she just LAUGHED!

I bet no one is laughing at your wall idea.

Good night from,

SAM

Dear Mr President,

I borrowed some books from the library to help me with my wall project. The Great Wall of China is humongous! Mum's favourite wall is the really old one in Zimbabwe. It was ten metres high and surrounded a whole kingdom! Hadrian's Wall went right across England and was 135 kilometres long!

My room is only four metres across – I don't understand why it's such a big deal.

Yours frustratedly,

SAM

Dear Mr President,

At school today my best friend, Robert Burns, told me you could see the Great Wall of China from space but Bella said that wasn't true.

I think I'll be an astronaut when I grow up, then I can see for myself.

Did you want to be a wall-builder when you were a kid?

All the best,

SAM

1 . . . . 2 . . . . 3 . . . . .

Dear Mr President,

I stayed with my grandma this weekend. It's great
staying there because I get my own room and Gran lets
me do pretty much whatever I want.

The downside was that there were some strange noises
in the night. I lay awake counting the walls between
my room and Gran's.

. . . . 4 . . . . , , 5 . . . . , ... 6

There's six. I counted them a lot of times.

Ciao for now,

Dear Mr President,

There has obviously been some 'dialogue' while
I was away. My brother is using words like 'harmony'
and 'spirit of sharing' and suggesting that a wall
is not needed.

I, however, remain unconvinced.

Laters,

-SAM

Dear Mr President,

I'm still the only one in the house who thinks
that the wall is a good idea.

I'm committed to getting it done even if my
big brother did 'ask' to borrow my robot
(he's <u>never</u> asked before) and last night he even
went under the covers to use his phone!

Best,

Sam

Dear Mr President,

I'm having second thoughts about the wall.
Yesterday, my brother put my clean washing on my bed
(he usually dumps it on the floor). I said thank you and
returned the cap I borrowed from him a few weeks ago.
Things are much better.

At dinner Dad said he was proud of us and told a very
long story about a wall in Berlin that got knocked down.
He said that communication and negotiation are always
preferable to separation.

I kind of see what he means.

See ya,

sam

Dear Mr President,

I'm really sorry but I'm dropping the whole wall idea.
To cut a long story short, a big brother in your room is
pretty cool when you've just had the worst nightmare ever.
I'm glad I hadn't got round to building it.

I feel a bit silly changing my mind but my brother says it's cool and Mum said she admires a man who admits when he's wrong.

Dad didn't say anything.

Anyway good luck with your wall.
Perhaps a small one would do?

Best wishes,

sam.

mister Tate's wall
(over next door)

More picture books from Templar:

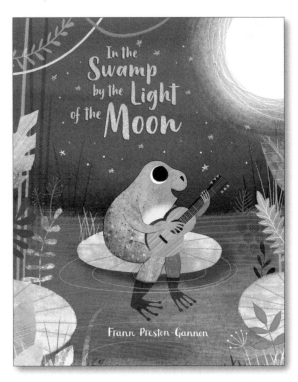

Paperback: 978-1-78741-386-3

Hardback: 978-1-78370-855-0
Paperback: 978-1-78370-870-3

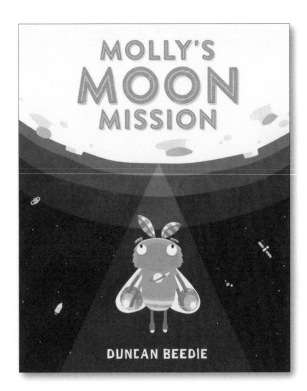

Paperback: 978-1-78741-340-5

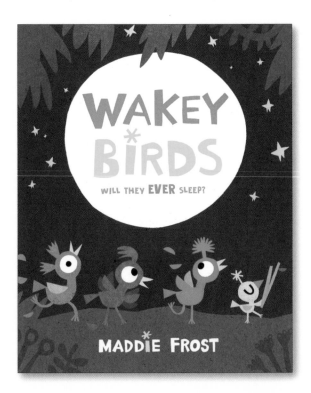

Paperback: 978-1-78741-366-5